GOING TO THE POOL

Written by Ena Keo   **Illustrated by Judith DuFour Love**

STECK-VAUGHN® COMPANY

ELEMENTARY • SECONDARY • ADULT • LIBRARY

 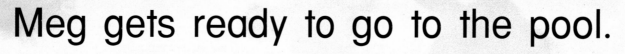

Meg gets ready to go to the pool.

2

Meg's dad is going to the pool, too.

3

 Andy gets ready to go to the pool.

Andy's mom is going to the pool, too.

 Rick gets ready to go to the pool.

Rick's mom is going to the pool, too.

 But no one gets into the pool.